S0-AFC-039

The Magic of Christmas
A Treasury of Holiday Stories
This edition produced 2007 for
BOOKS ARE FUN LTD
1680 Hwy 1 North, Fairfield, Iowa, IA 52556
by LITTLE TIGER PRESS
An imprint of Magi Publications
1 The Coda Centre, 189 Munster Road,
London SW6 6AW, UK
www.littletigerpress.com

This volume copyright © Magi Publications 2005
All rights reserved • ISBN 978-1-84506-654-3
Printed in China
2 4 6 8 10 9 7 5 3 1

I've Seen Santa!
David Bedford
Illustrated by Tim Warnes
First published in Great Britain 2005
by Little Tiger Press,
an imprint of Magi Publications
Text copyright © David Bedford 2005
Illustrations copyright © Tim Warnes 2005

Careful, Santa!
Julie Sykes
Illustrated by Tim Warnes
First published in Great Britain 2002
by Little Tiger Press,
an imprint of Magi Publications
Text copyright © Julie Sykes 2002
Illustrations copyright © Tim Warnes 2002

Laura's Christmas Star
Klaus Baumgart
English text by Judy Waite
First published in Great Britain 2000
by Little Tiger Press,
an imprint of Magi Publications
Originally published in Germany 1998
by Baumhaus Verlag, Frankfurt
Text and illustrations copyright
© Klaus Baumgart 1998
English text copyright © Little Tiger Press 1999

Ridiculous!
Michael Coleman
Illustrated by Gwyneth Williamson
First published in Great Britain 1996
by Little Tiger Press,
an imprint of Magi Publications
Text copyright © Michael Coleman 1996
Illustrations copyright
© Gwyneth Williamson 1996

Bless You, Santa!
Julie Sykes
Illustrated by Tim Warnes
First published in Great Britain 2004
by Little Tiger Press,
an imprint of Magi Publications
Text copyright © Julie Sykes 2004
Illustrations copyright © Tim Warnes 2004

The Gift of Christmas
Christine Leeson
Illustrated by Gaby Hansen
First published in Great Britain 2000
by Little Tiger Press,
an imprint of Magi Publications
Text copyright © Christine Leeson 2000
Illustrations copyright © Gaby Hansen 2000

The Magic of Christmas

A Treasury of Holiday Stories

Merry Christmas

LITTLE TIGER PRESS

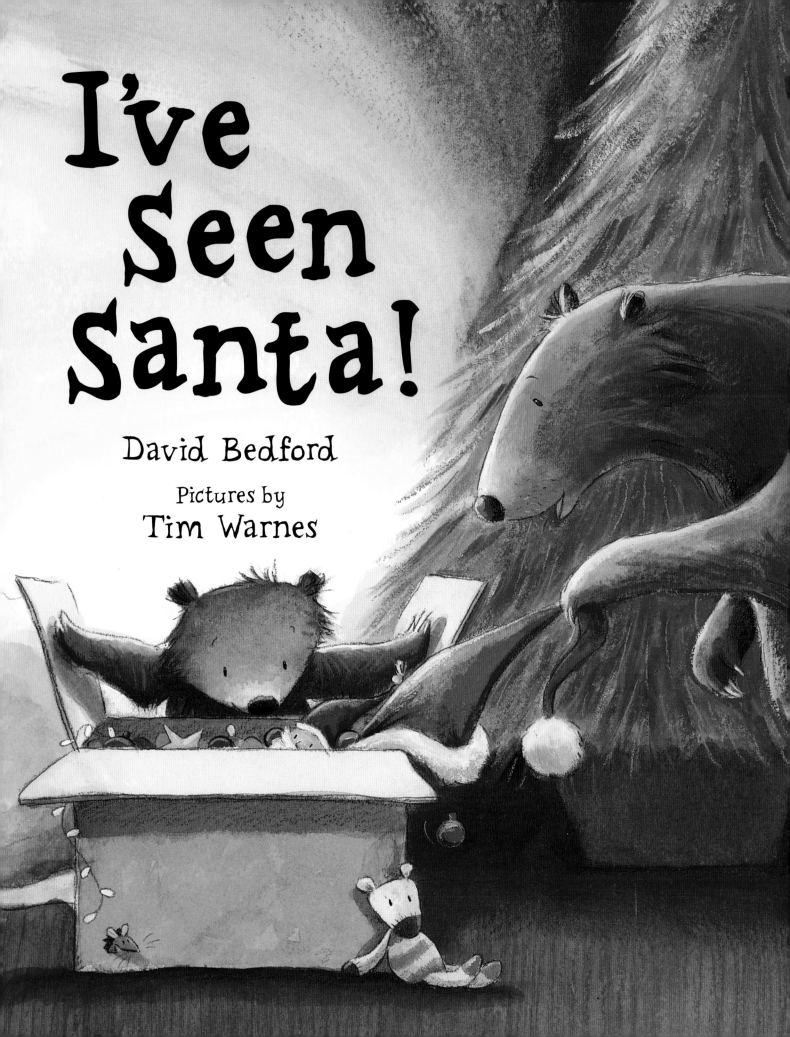

I've Seen Santa!

David Bedford

Pictures by
Tim Warnes

It was Christmas Eve,
and Little Bear was looking
forward to seeing Santa.
"Is Santa as big as you?"
he asked Big Bear.

"Nearly," said Big Bear, proudly.

"Oh," said Little Bear, looking worried. "Will Santa fit down our chimney, then?"

"Of course he will!" said Big Bear. "I'll show you."

Big Bear went outside and climbed into the chimney . . .

CRASH!

"See?" said Big Bear, from a cloud of soot.
"Santa will get in, no problem!"

"Santa won't come if he sees this mess!"
said Mommy Bear.
"We'll help clean up," said Little Bear.

"Does Santa visit bears
all over the world?"
said Little Bear.
"Yes," said Big Bear.
"He goes to every
house."

14

"Hmm," said Little Bear. "He might not have time to come here, and then I won't have any presents." "Don't worry," said Mommy Bear. "Santa will come just as soon as you go to sleep."

For SANTA
(paws off, Big Bear)

Little Bear didn't want to go to sleep.
He wanted to see Santa. He listened to
Mommy Bear and Big Bear going to bed.
And then . . . GLUG, GLUG, GLUG, GLUG!

What was that noise?
Someone was downstairs!

Someone big was sitting
by the fireplace.
"Yes!" whispered Little Bear.
"It's Santa! I've seen Santa!"
Little Bear tiptoed up and saw . . .

Big Bear!

"That's Santa's milk!" said Little Bear.

"I only wanted a sip," said Big Bear,
"before I go to sleep." He took Little
Bear's hand. "Come on, Little Bear.
Let's go to bed."

Little Bear tried to stay awake, but he soon began to doze.

Then a loud noise downstairs woke him up.

MUNCH! MUNCH! MUNCH! MUNCH!

Someone big was
standing by the
Christmas tree.
This time it had to be . . .

Big Bear again!

"You're eating Santa's blueberry
pies now!" said Little Bear.
   "I was hungry," said Big Bear.

"If Santa's as greedy as you,"
said Mommy Bear, coming
downstairs, "he really WILL
be too big to fit down the
chimney! Now go to bed
and go to sleep—
both of you!"

Little Bear went to bed, but he couldn't go to sleep. He was too worried. He woke up Big Bear to ask him a question.

"What if Santa eats too many blueberry pies and then gets stuck in the chimney?" he whispered.

"Hmm," said Big Bear.

"Let's keep watch to make sure he's OK," said Little Bear. "We can hide so he won't see us."

"Shhh!" whispered Little Bear
from their hiding place.
"I can hear something.
It MUST be Santa this time!"

26

Someone was putting
presents in their stockings!
Big Bear turned on his
flashlight to see . . .

Mommy Bear!

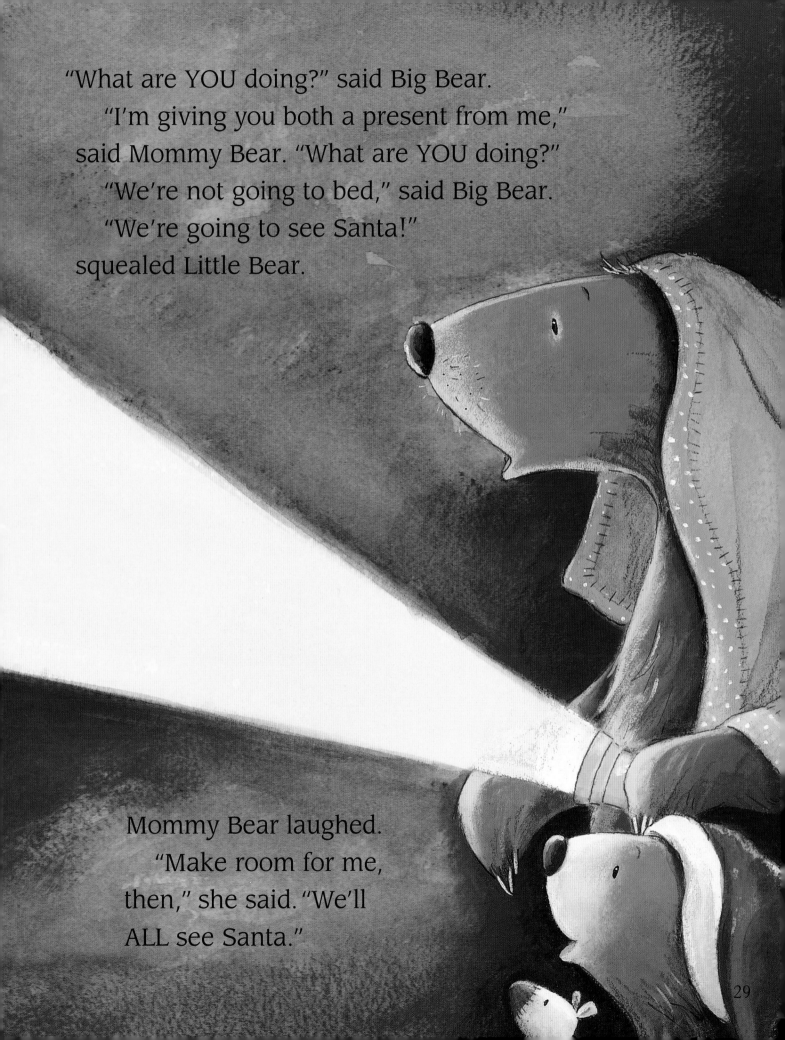

"What are YOU doing?" said Big Bear.

"I'm giving you both a present from me," said Mommy Bear. "What are YOU doing?"

"We're not going to bed," said Big Bear.

"We're going to see Santa!" squealed Little Bear.

Mommy Bear laughed. "Make room for me, then," she said. "We'll ALL see Santa."

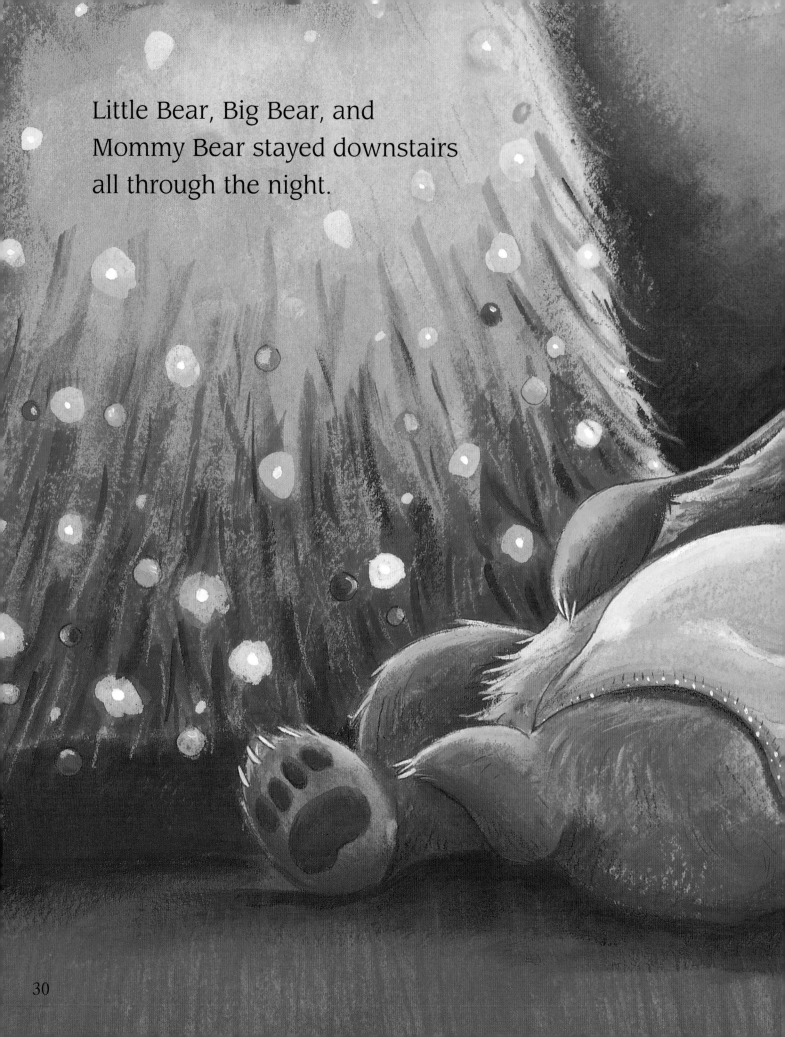

Little Bear, Big Bear, and
Mommy Bear stayed downstairs
all through the night.

But they never did see Santa . . .

even though
Santa saw them!

Careful, Santa!

North Pole

Julie Sykes
Tim Warnes

It was Christmas Eve and
Santa was loading presents
onto his sleigh. Santa's little
mouse was helping, too.
WHOOSH!
A gust of wind blew Santa's
beard straight in his face.
"Ho, ho, ho!" he chuckled.
"I can't see what I'm doing!"
"Careful, Santa!" warned
Santa's cat. "Don't lose
that bag of presents."

"That would be terrible!"
Santa agreed, as he carefully
placed the bag on the sleigh.

Santa helped his little mouse climb aboard
the sleigh.

"Hold on tight!" he boomed. "We're off!"

It was a wild and windy night.

"Oh my!" shouted Santa, as the sleigh
rocked this way and that. Suddenly, the bag
of presents began to move.

"Careful, Santa!" called Santa's little mouse.

"Watch those presents!"

But Santa wasn't quick enough. The bag of presents
slid across the sleigh and toppled overboard.
"Stop!" cried Santa in alarm. "Down, reindeer, down!
I've lost all the presents!"

The reindeer struggled
against the wind . . .

and landed as gently as they could.
"Careful, Santa!" they shouted, but it
was too late . . .
"WHOOPS!" cried Santa, landing on
his bottom.

Santa scrambled to his feet.
The presents were scattered far and
wide and he hurried to pick them up.
He didn't notice the frozen pond.

"Whee!" cried Santa,
as he slid across the ice toward
the duck house.

46

"Careful, Santa!" quacked the ducks.
"You nearly squashed us."
"How awful," said Santa as he picked
up the presents. "Sorry about that.
Has anyone seen my present bag?"

"Here it is!" chattered a squirrel from high in a tree. Santa bravely climbed up, but before he knew it he was stuck in the branches. "Oh, help!" he cried.

"Careful, Santa!"
called the squirrel.
"I am trying to
be careful," said Santa,
as he struggled to get free.
Very slowly, Santa climbed
back down, dropping
some presents as he went.

At the playground, a few presents were lying under the swings. Santa put them into his bag, then he spotted some more on the slide.

"Whoosh!" cried Santa, as he zoomed down the slide.

"Careful, Santa, you're going too fast!" warned Santa's cat.

"Eek! I can't stop!" said Santa, as he slid toward a snowman.

"Sorry, snowman, I didn't mean to bump you," Santa said, as he dusted himself off and popped the last of the presents into his bag.

"That's it!" he boomed. "It's time to
deliver these presents. Ready, mouse?"
But where was Santa's mouse?
Santa couldn't see her anywhere.
"Oh dear!" he cried. "First I lose
my bag of presents, and now
I've lost my little mouse.
This is horrible."

The ducks, the squirrel, and Santa's cat all
crowded around.
"Don't worry, Santa!" they chattered. "She
can't be very far. We'll help you look for her."

Everyone looked for Santa's mouse.
She wasn't in the duck house.
She wasn't near the slide or behind
the snowman.

Just then, Santa heard a
familiar squeak. He shined
his flashlight up . . .

55

and there was his mouse, hanging from a branch in a tree.
"Careful!" warned Santa. "It's far too windy to play
up there. That branch doesn't look too safe to me."

But the mouse wasn't playing. "I'm stuck," she squeaked. "Please get me down!" Quickly, Santa took off his jacket and spread it out on the ground. Everyone gathered round and held the coat like a trampoline. "Hold on tight, everyone, and don't let go!" said Santa.

"Ready, mouse?
One, two, three . . .

JUMP!"

Mouse jumped and, with a bounce and a plop,
she landed safely on Santa's coat.
"Hooray!" cheered Santa. "Thank you, everyone."

It was time to go. Santa and his mouse
hurried to their sleigh.
"Reindeer, up, up, and away!" cried Santa.
Whoosh! blew the wind.

"Careful, Santa," called everyone,
as the sleigh rocked this way and that.
"Look after that mouse, and HOLD
ON TIGHT TO THOSE PRESENTS!"

Laura's
Christmas Star

Klaus Baumgart

English text by Judy Waite

"Do you believe in magic?" asked Tommy, watching Laura pack her suitcase. They were going to Aunt Martha's for Christmas this year. Laura smiled. It was a quiet, secret smile.

"Sometimes," she said.

"Aunt Martha says her Christmas tree looks magical," Tommy went on. "She says it's huge and sparkly and it glitters like a zillion stars. I can't *wait* to see it."

"Are you packed?" asked Mom, coming into the room. She gave them both a hug. "It's time for bed now. Otherwise you'll both be tired and grumpy on the journey to Aunt Martha's tomorrow."

Laura closed her eyes, letting pictures of a zillion
glittery stars float into her thoughts.
"Is it morning yet?" asked Tommy.
Laura opened one eye.
"We've only just gone to bed," she said. "Go back
to sleep."
Laura closed her eyes again and thought of huge
sparkly Christmas trees and colorful wrapping.
"Is it time to get up yet?" asked Tommy.
"No," said Laura. "It's still the middle of the night."
Ten minutes passed. It seemed like ten years to Tommy.
"Is it morning *now?*" asked Tommy, nudging Laura awake.
Laura opened both her eyes. She seemed to have slept
a long time. "I think it must be," she said.

Laura and Tommy jumped up, pulled on their clothes,
and ran into Mom and Dad's bedroom.

"It's not time to get up," groaned Mom, waking up.

"Go back to bed!"

Laura and Tommy wandered back to their room, but they
didn't go to bed. They sat by the window, staring out at
the zillions of sparkly, glittering stars.

"Look!" cried Tommy, pointing. "That star's brighter than
the others."

Laura smiled her secret smile. The bright star was her own,
special, magic star. She had once rescued it when it had
fallen from the sky. When it was better, she had set it free.
Though it was now far away, she knew it was her friend.

71

At last morning came. Laura and Tommy helped Mom and Dad pack the car. Nearby on the sidewalk a man was selling Christmas trees. He waved at them and shouted "Merry Christmas!" "We're going to spend Christmas at Aunt Martha's," Tommy shouted back. "She's got a Christmas tree that's huge and sparkly and glitters like a zillion stars."

At last they were off. The sky began to turn all gray and soft. It looked as if it was going to snow.

73

As they reached the country, beautiful snowflakes began to
drift down. Laura and Tommy pressed their noses against the
car window and watched them cover the earth like icing
on a Christmas cake.

Suddenly the car began to rattle. It began to cough.

"It sounds like it's got a bad cold," said Laura.

"It sounds like it's broken down," said Mom.

Everyone got out, and Dad opened up the hood.

He pulled at some wires, but he didn't get the
car started.

Everyone climbed back into the car and waited for the repairman to arrive. It grew colder and colder, and everyone huddled together to keep warm. Dad tried singing Christmas songs and telling jokes, but the songs sounded flat, and the jokes weren't funny.

"I'll tell you a story," said Laura. "It's about a magic Christmas star that saves everybody."

But as she started, Tommy began to cry. "There's no such thing as magic," he whispered sadly. "We'll *never* get to Aunt Martha's now. I'll never see her huge sparkly Christmas tree that glitters like a zillion stars."

By the time the repairman had
fixed the car, it was too late to go to Aunt Martha's.
Tommy tried not to cry as Dad drove back home and
78   they carried their suitcases into the house.

Tommy stayed sad as the daylight faded and the night
crept back into the sky.

"I wish I could do something to make Tommy happy again,"
Laura whispered. She looked out of her bedroom, and her
special star appeared. It shone down at her, as if it
understood Tommy's sadness.

The man who had been selling Christmas trees was long
gone, but suddenly Laura noticed that he had left behind a
little tree. It lay in the snow looking ragged and battered,
and very lonely. "I'll get it for Tommy," Laura cried. "Maybe
it will cheer him up."

Laura ran outside to where the little tree
was lying. "Come indoors with me," she
said. "You look awfully lonely out here
on your own."

Laura carried the tree into the house.

"Thanks for getting it," said Tommy sadly. "It's a nice little tree. But it's not very sparkly, is it? It's not very glittery."

Laura looked at the tree. Tommy was right.

It could never be like the magical tree Aunt Martha had promised them.

Laura went upstairs to sit by her window. At least she could tell her star how helpless she felt. It always listened to her and understood. But as she looked into the night sky, she gasped with horror. Her special star had disappeared!

Now Laura was as sad as Tommy. There wasn't much
to feel happy about now she had lost a special friend.
And maybe Tommy was right. Maybe there was no
such thing as magic after all.

Suddenly, she heard Dad calling to them.

"Laura, Tommy, come here quickly!"

Puzzled, the two children trailed downstairs.

"Look!" gasped Mom, as they all stood by the
living-room door.

Laura and Tommy looked. They couldn't believe
what they were seeing.

"It's *wonderful!*" cried Tommy, turning to Laura with
shining eyes. "But how could it have happened?"

Laura smiled her quiet, secret smile.
She knew, of course. "It must be magic,"
she said.

Ridiculous!

Michael Coleman

Pictures by Gwyneth Williamson

"Ho hum," yawned Mr. Tortoise. "Winter is here."
"So it is," yawned Mrs. Tortoise. "Come on,
Shelley, time for bed."

"But I don't feel sleepy yet," said Shelley.

"*Ridiculous!*" cried Mr. Tortoise. "All tortoises
go to sleep for the winter."
"Why?" asked Shelley.
"Because it's cold outside and there's no food."

"But I don't want to go to sleep," said Shelley.
"I want to see what winter is like!"
"*Ridiculous!*" cried Mr. and Mrs. Tortoise together.
"Whoever heard of a tortoise outside in winter?"

Soon
Mr. Tortoise
began to snore...

and not long after
that Mrs. Tortoise
began to snore...

98

...and not long after *that*, Shelley left her warm
bed of leaves, and out she went through a hole in
the shed to see what winter was like.

Outside the shed, Shelley blinked.
There was snow and ice everywhere,
even on the duck pond and the hill. As
she lumbered along, a duck spotted her.

"A tortoise out in winter?" quacked the duck.
"*Ridiculous!*"

"No it isn't," said Shelley.

"Oh no? Then let's see you break through the
ice to get food like *I* can. Ha-quack-ha!"

"He's right," thought Shelley. "I can't do that.
I don't have a beak."

As Shelley began to walk up the hill,
she met a dog.

"A tortoise out in winter?" barked the dog. "*Ridiculous!*"

"No it isn't," said Shelley, feeling a bit cross.

"Oh no? Then let's see you keep warm by running around like *I* can. Ha-woof-ha!"

"He's right," thought Shelley sadly. "I can't do that either."

The dog ran off after a cat, but the cat
jumped on to the branch of a tree.
She looked down at Shelley.

"A tortoise out in winter?" meowed the cat.
"*Ridiculous!*"

"No it isn't," said Shelley, even more crossly.

"Oh no? Then let's see you run into a nice warm house as quickly as *I* can. Ha-meow-ha!"

"She's right," thought Shelley, shivering with cold.

"I can't run like a dog or a cat. I'm much too slow!"

The cat raced off into her house before the dog could catch her, and Shelley trudged toward the top of the hill, where she met a bird.

"A tortoise out in winter?" cheeped the bird.
"*Ridiculous!*"
"No it isn't," snapped Shelley.
"Oh no? Then let's see you fly home
 and cuddle up with your family like *I* can.
 Ha-cheep-ha!"
"Of course I can't fly," thought Shelley.
"I can't even hop!"

Shelley felt cold and miserable. She remembered her warm, cozy bed, and a tear trickled down her cheek. "They're *all* right," she thought. "A tortoise out in winter *is* ridiculous!"

She was so sad she didn't notice the big patch of ice ahead...

...and she slipped on it!
Shelley fell over backward, and began to slide
down the hill.
Faster and faster she went...

...faster than
a *dog* could run...

...faster than
a *cat*...

...until suddenly she hit a bump...

...and flew into the air like a *bird*.

Wheeee!
With a thump Shelley landed on the
icy duck pond and slid toward the hole
in the shed...

...but it was all covered up with ice!
"Ha-quack-ha, what did I say?" cried
the duck as she slid by him. "Where's
your beak to break the ice with?"
"I don't have a beak," thought Shelley.
"But I *do* have...

…a shell!"
And tucking her head inside it,
she broke through the ice,
into the shed and home!

Hearing all the noise, Mrs. Tortoise woke up.
"You haven't been outside, have you, Shelley?"
she asked.

"A tortoise out in winter?" said Shelley,
snuggling into bed. And before she could say
"*Ridiculous!*"
she was fast asleep.

Bless You, Santa!

Julie Sykes   Tim Warnes

It was almost Christmas, and Santa
was up very early one day.

"Jingle bells, jingle bells," he sang to himself.
"Breakfast first and then to work."

He made some toast and took out the
jam and butter. As he was pouring some cereal,
though, his nose began to tickle.

"*Aah, aah, aah . . .*"

122

"Achoooo!"

he roared. His sneeze blew the
cereal all over the place!

"Bless you, Santa," said Santa's cat, shaking cereal out of her tail. "That's a nasty cold."

"Oh, no!" said Santa in alarm. "It can't be. It's nearly Christmas. I don't have time for a cold."

After breakfast Santa rushed to his workshop and went to work on the unfinished toys. Happily he sang as he painted a robot. But Santa's sneezes were growing larger and louder.

"*Aah, aah, aah…*"

"Achoooo!"

"Bless you, Santa," squeaked
Santa's little mouse, gathering the beads
his sneezes had scattered across the table.

"Bless you, Santa," said Santa's cat, chasing paper stars as they fluttered around. "You sound awful. Go and sit by the fire."

"I feel awful!" said Santa. "But I can't rest yet. It's too close to Christmas. I have to finish these toys or there will be no presents for all the . . . *aah, aah, aah . . .*"

"Achoooo!"

Santa sneezed so hard that he
slipped and landed in a pile of balls.
Down the balls tumbled, bouncing off
Santa and bouncing around the room.
They crashed into cars, they pushed over
paint cans, they toppled the teddy bears,
and they ruined the rockets.

"Achoooo!

"Just look at this mess!" cried Santa. "I'll never be ready in time for Christmas."

"Go to bed, Santa," ordered Santa's little mouse. "You're not well. Your nose is so red the reindeer could use it to guide your sleigh. We'll clean up this mess and get everything ready for Christmas."

133

So Santa's mouse put Santa to bed with
a mug of hot tea and a little medicine
to help his cold.
   Santa snuggled into the blanket.
He sneezed.

"Achoooo!"

He sniffled . . .

And finally he snored.

Meanwhile, back in the workshop,
Santa's friends worked as hard as they
could. They mopped.

They mended.

They glued.

They snipped, they stuck, and they wrapped.
Faster and faster they worked until every
single present was finished. Then sleepily
they went to bed.

The next evening, as the sun set, the animals waited with a sleigh piled high with toys.

"But where is Santa?" asked Santa's cat. "I hope he's better."

"Who's going to drive the sleigh and deliver all the presents?" asked the reindeer.

"Listen," said Santa's cat. "Can you hear something?"

The animals listened.

"It's Santa!" squeaked Santa's little mouse. "Are you better, Santa? Can you deliver the presents?"

Santa wrinkled his nose. *"Aah, aah, aah . . ."*

"Ho, ho, ho!" chuckled Santa loudly.

"Only joking! I feel much better. Bless you, everyone. You did a great job! Thanks to you I will get these presents delivered in time for Christmas morning."

Santa climbed aboard his sleigh. "Reindeer, up, up, and away!" he shouted.

It was a busy night as Santa flew
around the world delivering presents.

When at last Santa landed back at the North Pole the sun was rising. But he hadn't finished yet.

"These presents are for you," said Santa.

"Presents for us!" squeaked Santa's cat. *"Th . . .th . . . thaa . . ."*

"Achoooo!"

Santa's cat sneezed so hard that a pile of
snow fell off the trees and buried everyone.
"Bless you!" laughed Santa. "And merry
Christmas to you, too!"

144

THE GIFT OF
CHRISTMAS

by Christine Leeson
Pictures by Gaby Hansen

It was Molly Mouse's first Christmas. The sky was streaked with pink and gold, and there was a tingle in the air.

Through the window of a house something was shining and glittering into the night.

"What is that, Mom?" asked Molly.

"It's a Christmas tree," said her mother. "People cover it with shiny balls, lights, and stars."

"I wish *we* had a Christmas tree," sighed Molly.

"Why don't you go into the woods to find one?" said her mother. "You could make it look just as nice as that tree in the window."

Molly thought this was a great idea. She called her brothers and sisters together, and off they all scampered.

On the way to the woods, they came to a barn. The mice rummaged through it, looking for something to add to their tree. Under a big pile of hay, Molly found a doll.

"This is like the doll on the top of the Christmas tree in the window," she said. "It will be just right for our tree."

But the doll belonged to someone else.
"Grr!" said the old farm dog. "That's mine!"
"Don't chase us!" cried Molly. "I only thought
the doll would look nice on our Christmas tree."
The old dog yawned. It was true that sometimes
he chased mice. But because it was Christmas,
or because he remembered the Christmas tree
in the farmhouse and how he used to play
with the children there, he said the mice
could borrow the doll.

The mice left the barn and walked across
the barnyard, carrying the doll. They came to
the edge of the woods.
"Hey," Molly shouted. "I see something else
we can put on our Christmas tree!" It was a
gold ribbon, hanging from a branch of an oak
tree. Molly scampered up the trunk, took hold
of the ribbon, and pulled.

But the ribbon belonged to a magpie.
She had taken it to line her nest.
"Please don't be angry," said Molly.
"I only wanted the gold ribbon for
our Christmas tree."

Usually the magpie chased mice. But because
it was Christmas, or because she had also been
admiring the Christmas tree in the window, she
let go of the other end of the ribbon. Molly took
the ribbon thankfully.

In the distance Molly saw some shiny round things
lying on the ground. They were like the shiny balls
on the Christmas tree in the window.
"Exactly what we want!" cried Molly, running
to pick one of them up. "Now we have a doll, a
gold ribbon, and a shiny ball!"

But those shiny balls belonged to a fox. "Those
are my crab apples," he barked. "I'm saving them
for the cold days ahead."
"We only thought one would look good on our
Christmas tree," said Molly, trembling.
The fox sniffed. He chased mice most of the time.
But because it was Christmas, or because he had
never seen a Christmas tree before, he went back
into the woods. Molly picked up a shiny crab
apple and carried it away.

Twilight was falling as the mice went deeper into the woods. There, in the middle of a bramble bush, they could see a shining star and a dozen tiny lights glittering green and gold.

"Stars for our tree!" shouted Molly. "Let me get them." But when Molly reached into the bush, she found not stars . . .

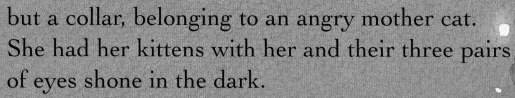

but a collar, belonging to an angry mother cat.
She had her kittens with her and their three pairs
of eyes shone in the dark.

"Oh no!" gulped Molly. "I only wanted something
sparkly for our Christmas tree."

The cat pricked her ears. She always chased mice.
But because it was Christmas, or because she
remembered the Christmas tree in the cozy home
where she'd been a kitten, the mother cat slipped
off her collar. She let the mice have it for their tree.

At last, in a clearing in the deepest
part of the woods, the mice found
a large evergreen tree.
"Our Christmas tree!"
cried Molly. They hung the
doll, the ribbon, the crab apple,
and the cat's collar on the
tree's branches.

"Oh," said Molly when they had finished. "It doesn't look at all like the tree I saw in the window." Sadly the mice turned away. Disappointed, they walked all the way back home and went straight to bed.

In the middle of the night the mother mouse woke up
Molly and her brothers and sisters. "Come with me,"
she whispered. "I have something to show you."
The mice scurried along behind their mother, past the
farm and into the woods. Other animals hurried on
ahead of them, into the deepest part of the woods.

At last the mice reached the clearing
where Molly's Christmas tree was.
Molly stood completely still. Her eyes
grew large and round.
"Oh, look at that!" she cried.

During the night the animals had all added decorations to the Christmas tree. The frost had come and touched everything with glitter. The little tree sparkled, and even the stars in the sky seemed to be caught in its branches, with the biggest and brightest star right at the very top.

"Our Christmas tree is even better than the one in the window," whispered Molly happily. And because it was Christmas, all the animals from the woods sat quietly around the tree, at peace with each other.